THE
WORLD'S
MOST

WORLD'S MOST
EXTREME
ANIMALS

—

Karen McGhee

Gareth Stevens
PUBLISHING

Please visit our website, www.garethstevens.com. For a free color catalog of all our high-quality books, call toll free 1-800-542-2595 or fax 1-877-542-2596.

Cataloging-in-Publication Data

Names: McGhee, Karen.
Title: World's most extreme animals / Karen McGhee.
Description: New York : Gareth Stevens, 2022. | Series: The world's most | Includes glossary and index.
Identifiers: ISBN 9781538274675 (pbk.) | ISBN 9781538274699 (library bound) | ISBN 9781538274682 (6 pack) | ISBN 9781538274705 (ebook)
Subjects: LCSH: Animals–Miscellanea–Juvenile literature. | Animal behavior–Juvenile literature. | Animals–Juvenile literature.
Classification: LCC QL49.M385 2022 | DDC 590–dc23

World's Most Extreme: © 2017 by Australian Geographic,
an imprint of Australian Geographic Holdings Pty Ltd.

Published in 2022 by
Gareth Stevens Publishing
29 E. 21st Street
New York, NY 10010

Editor: Lauren Smith
Book design: Katherine McKinnon

Printed in the United States of America

CPSIA compliance information: Batch #CWGS22: For further information contact Gareth Stevens, New York, New York at 1-800-542-2595.

Find us on

CONTENTS

MASSIVE MOLARS

GIANT PANDA

Although giant pandas have a largely vegetarian diet and eat mostly bamboo, they are actually classified scientifically as carnivores, which are meat-eating animals. As a result of their bamboo-chomping lifestyle, pandas have evolved the biggest molar teeth of any carnivore. These, along with their strong jaws, allow them to crush hard bamboo stems as big as 1.5 inches (4 cm) wide.

FAST FACT

Because bamboo has such low nutrient levels, adult pandas need to each eat about 44 pounds (20 kg) a day. That can take them 16 hours to eat.

LARGEST AMPHIBIAN

CHINESE GIANT SALAMANDER

This huge relative of frogs and toads can grow to be almost 6 feet (1.8 m) long. But, sadly, there are very few left now and they are rarely seen at that size.

EXTINCTION THREAT

The Chinese giant salamander is critically endangered due partly to hunting for use in traditional Chinese medicine.

LARGEST SPIDER

1 foot (30 cm) long

GIANT HUNTSMAN SPIDER

The famous goliath birdeater might be the largest spider when measured by weight, but the giant huntsman spider takes the prize when it comes to sheer size. This spider was only discovered in 2001, in a cave in the southeastern Asian country of Laos, which lies north of Thailand. If this slender spider species sat on a dinner plate, its legs would stretch right across. No other spider has such a leg span: up to 1 foot (30 cm).

MOST EYES

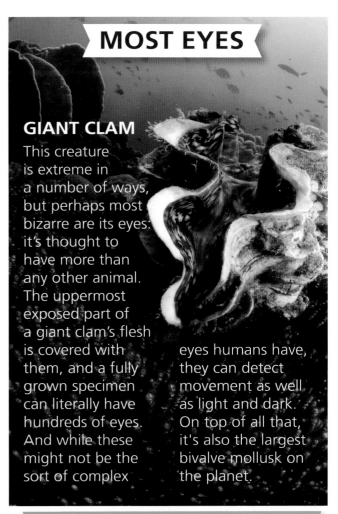

GIANT CLAM

This creature is extreme in a number of ways, but perhaps most bizarre are its eyes: it's thought to have more than any other animal. The uppermost exposed part of a giant clam's flesh is covered with them, and a fully grown specimen can literally have hundreds of eyes. And while these might not be the sort of complex eyes humans have, they can detect movement as well as light and dark. On top of all that, it's also the largest bivalve mollusk on the planet.

SMALLEST MAMMAL

BUMBLEBEE BAT

This tiny furred creature weighs less than some insects. In fact, this species is about as small as a mammal can be, as being warm-blooded at this tiny size requires a huge amount of energy. These bats weigh less than an ounce with a head and body length of only about 1 inch (25 mm).

FACT BOX — SMALL SHREWS

The bumblebee bat is the smallest mammal by absolute size, but the Etruscan shrew happens to weigh a tiny bit less.

ASIA

WEIRDEST TUSKS

NORTH SULAWESI BABIRUSA

It's well-known that the tusks on elephants and rhinos and the antlers of deer and antelope are weapons, used against predators and to spar against males of the same species.

But no one is quite sure about the purpose of the tusks on a male babirusa, though they are thought to potentially protect their eyes. These extraordinary features are actually upper canine teeth that grow out from the jaw and through the nose to curve back towards the forehead. The lower canines of a male babirusa are also sharp and protruding. There are four babirusa species, all found in Indonesia. The North Sulawesi species is the largest and can grow tusks to a length of more than 15 inches (40 cm), which eventually repenetrate the skull.

FACT BOX — USELESS WEAPONS

Bubirusa tusks are so brittle that they break off easily, making them useless as weapons or for any purpose other than display.

LONGEST GESTATION PERIOD

ASIAN ELEPHANT

All elephant species have an exceptionally long gestation period (the full length of an average pregnancy). Elephant moms are pregnant for 20.5 to 22 months, which is nearly two years and longer than any other animal. That's more than twice as long as the human gestation period of 9 months. Despite being smaller than its African relatives, the average Asian elephant's gestation period is just a little bit longer, ahead by a few days.

WIDEST CRAB

13 feet (4 m) long

JAPANESE SPIDER CRAB

When it comes to width, no crab is bigger than the Japanese spider crab, which is found mostly in deep waters in the Pacific Ocean off the coast of Japan. Although the carapace (the shell covering the main body) of these crabs is usually no longer than about 15 inches (37 cm), the leg span of adults can be massive—as wide as 13 feet (4 m), which is wider than a bus! The Japanese spider crab can weigh up to 44 pounds (20 kg).

AMAZING POWERS OF REGENERATION

ZEBRAFISH

Scientists are looking to the small freshwater zebrafish from the Himalayas to learn how to fix broken hearts. Zebrafish are vertebrates, with a heart a lot like ours. But they have a very special and unique capability for regeneration. When a zebrafish heart is wounded, the site is quickly sealed off by a clot and the surrounding heart muscle slowly grows over it. Soon the heart is almost as good as new and pumping just as strongly as ever.

FASTEST FISH

BLACK MARLIN

The Indo-Pacific sailfish is at the top of the fastest fish list, as it's been recorded slicing through the tropical waters of the Indian and Pacific Oceans at speeds of more than 68 miles (110 km) per hour in short bursts. More recently, however, another fish has laid claim to the title of fastest fish. Based on the rate at which hooked black marlins unwind fishing line from a reel, scientists have estimated that this fish can reach a top speed of 80 miles (129 km) per hour.

LONGEST REPTILE

RETICULATED PYTHON

Southeast Asia's reticulated python doesn't get as heavy as South America's anaconda, but it certainly seems to grow longer. There have been many reports of individuals longer than 19 feet (6 m) and the longest officially documented individual was 25.1 feet (7.67 m). In 2016, a specimen was caught on the Malaysian island of Penang that was estimated to be 26 feet (8 m).

26 feet (8 m) long

FASTEST PUNCH AND AMAZING EYESIGHT

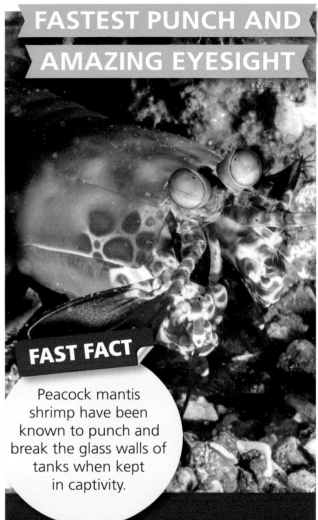

FAST FACT

Peacock mantis shrimp have been known to punch and break the glass walls of tanks when kept in captivity.

PEACOCK MANTIS SHRIMP

The peacock mantis shrimp is a stunning-looking creature that has two extreme claims to fame. First, this colorful crustacean has a dark side: it likes to punch and it does so at a startling 50 miles (80 km) per hour—faster than any other animal. It has two front claws specially adapted for punching through the tough shells of mollusks to reach the soft tissue inside, which it eats.

The other astounding feature of peacock mantis shrimps is their eyesight. They have highly specialized eyes that can see color better than most animals, including humans. Even more impressive is that they can also detect several different types of light, including infrared and ultraviolet light and even a type of polarized light that no other animal is known to be able to detect.

EUROPE

The sperm whale has another extreme feature: It has an 18-pound (8 kg) brain, the largest of any animal that has ever lived.

LOUDEST ANIMAL

SPERM WHALE

The animal kingdom is full of squawking, screeching, rumbling loudmouths, but the loudest of them all is the sperm whale. These huge deep-ocean creatures appear to be able to communicate by producing clicking noises, the loudest of which have been measured at 230 **decibels** (dB). To give you an idea of how loud this is, a jet airplane taking off is about 165 dB. Sperm whale clicks are quick (no more than 30 milliseconds) but they can be heard by another sperm whale more than 10 miles (16 km) away.

HIGH-DENSITY DWELLER

JUMPING APPARATUS

Most springtail species have a jumping organ called a furcula attached to their abdomens.

SPRINGTAILS

Ever feel that you're not alone? Chances are you never have been. The world is crawling with life, and we're not just talking bacteria or other microscopic flora and fauna. Among the most abundant creatures in the world are insect-like creatures called springtails. With most less than an inch long, many different types are visible to the naked eye, if you look out for them. Springtails live in high humidity environments, where they feed on substances such as mold, bacteria, and decaying plant matter. Scientists estimate their numbers to be as high as 100,000 per 35 cubic feet (1 cu m), even in places where they live with people.

FOUR-HEARTED FISH

HAGFISH

Hagfish are ancient fish with four hearts, part of a primitive system that circulates blood around their bodies. One heart acts as the main pump while the other three help out. Another extreme hagfish feature is how they eat: They burrow deep into the dead bodies of other animals to eat their rotting flesh from the inside out. Then there's their response to **predators**. When something tries to grab them, they produce such huge quantities of slime that they're impossible to get hold of.

MOST BRAIN CELLS

LONG-FINNED PILOT WHALE

The neocortex is a part of the brain that is particularly well developed in humans. Neuroscientists had always assumed we had more nerve cells in the neocortex than any other species. They got a shock in 2014 when a study of the brains of long-finned pilot whales in the North Atlantic found that this species has more brain cells in the neocortex than any other species ever studied, and almost twice as many neurons in this part of the brain as humans. Scientists are still wrestling with what this might mean about the intelligence of pilot whales.

LARGEST INVERTEBRATE

GIANT SQUID

There's no doubt the giant squid is certainly the largest invertebrate alive today, but no one is quite sure just *how* big it gets. Suspected to be the cause of many sea monster myths, this enormous mollusk species is rarely seen as it lives at great depths in the Atlantic Ocean where it feeds on deep-sea fishes and squid. But there have been reports of specimens 60 feet (18 m) long washing ashore.

EUROPE

ARCTIC TERN

These small birds embark on a huge annual **migration** that takes them around the planet and back, further than any other bird. Every year they fly from breeding grounds in the Arctic to the other end of the world to spend the summer in the Southern Hemisphere, feeding on small fish and crustaceans in waters off Antarctica, then fly back again. It's a return journey that can take them, on average, across more than 43,500 miles (70,000 km). They're long-lived birds and many will complete this return trip more than 20 times during their lifetime.

FAST FACT

Most Arctic terns return to breed at the same place, and usually in the same colony, where they themselves hatched.

ONLY COLOR-CHANGING DOG

ARCTIC FOX

The Arctic fox is the only member of the dog family that changes its coat color as the weather warms. It's white for much of the year when its habitat is also shrouded in white snow, and it needs to be **camouflaged** so that it can sneak up on its prey. But as the snow and ice melts in spring and summer, and the Arctic tundra is transformed by darker tones, the head, legs, tail, and back of the Arctic fox turn brown while its sides and underbelly take on lighter tones.

LONGEST-LIVING VERTEBRATE

GREENLAND SHARK

Found mostly in deep waters off the North Atlantic and Arctic oceans, the Greenland shark is thought to live longer than any other vertebrate. By counting layers of proteins in the lens of the eyes of female sharks caught in nets, scientists estimated that this huge fish can live for more than 400 years. It's known that female Greenland sharks can't reproduce until after they reach 13 feet (4 m) in length, which means they must be about 150 years old before they produce their first young!

LONGEST ANIMAL

BOOTLACE WORM

The bootlace worm, a marine invertebrate found in sediment along the British coast, could make the cut as the world's longest animal. Specimens are often found between 16 to 50 feet (5 to 15 m) long, but can reach much greater lengths, with reports of individuals that can be stretched out to 180 feet (55 m), longer than any other creature.

DEEPEST AND LONGEST DIVER

CUVIER'S BEAKED WHALE

No other mammal dives deeper or longer than Cuvier's beaked whale. Using **satellite tags** to track whales off the California coast, scientists have recorded adults of this species diving to depths of almost 1.8 miles (3 km) during dives of longer than two hours. Exactly how these whales manage to navigate and withstand the immense pressure at these sorts of depths is not yet fully understood. But they're thought to have collapsible rib cages to reduce air pockets that would make them buoyant as they dive.

ONLY ANIMAL TO LIVE FOREVER

IMMORTAL JELLYFISH

Life for this jellyfish species begins, as it does for all jellyfish, as a larva that swims about in the **plankton**. Unlike most other jellyfish, however, this larvae ultimately settles down onto the sea floor to develop into a colony of attached creatures known as polyps. From these, free-swimming jellyfish bud off and reach adulthood in a matter of weeks and at a size of less than a quarter inch. If, however, these are threatened or injured in any way, they revert back to the polyp stage and create a new colony from which new adults are budded. This cycle can go on indefinitely. It's as if the jellyfish can simply press a reset button every time life gets tough!

MOST DISGUSTING BIRD

NORTHERN FULMAR

Fulmar chicks are as fluffy and cute as any other baby bird, but they're certainly not as defenseless. Their response to a potential threat or predator is to vomit up a vile orange-colored concoction from deep in their gut, which they shoot up to 6 feet (1.8 m). This acts as a deterrent because it smells disgustingly of rotten fish and also because it is so sticky that it's almost impossible to remove, even with repeated scrubbing.

AFRICA

SMARTEST ANIMAL

CHIMPANZEE

There are many different ways to measure intelligence and different animals are smart in different ways. But scientists continue to be astounded by the intellect of the chimpanzee, one of the species most closely related to humans. Dutch primatologist Fras de Waal named a chimp called Ayumu as number one on his list of smart animals because he outperformed humans on a memory test. They are also known to learn words, use tools, and play with objects.

MOST ABUNDANT BIRD

RED-BILLED QUELEA

This small brown finch lives on Africa's **savanna** and doesn't look like anything extraordinary. In fact it looks a lot like a common sparrow. But it likes hanging with other red-billed queleas so much that it can form super-colonies of up to 30 million birds. Each quelea can eat half its body weight in grain per day, which is about 0.3 ounce (10 g) of grain, meaning that a flock of two million birds can devour up to 22 tons (20 mt) of grain in a single day. It's for this reason that, as well as being the world's most abundant bird, the red-billed quelea has another claim to fame: one of Africa's most hated birds! Its huge flocks are able to decimate entire fields of crops within hours.

FAST FACT

The estimated breeding population of red-billed queleas is 1.5 billion birds.

LARGEST SNAIL

AFRICAN GIANT SNAIL

No other slug or snail gets bigger than this massive mollusk. The largest African giant snail ever recorded was 15.5 inches (39.3 cm) long, from the end of its outstretched tail to the tip of its snout— longer than a school ruler. It weighed almost 2 pounds (900 g) and had a shell 10.7 inches (27.3 cm) long. These invertebrates are vegetarians, munching on plant matter, living or dead, at night in their forest habitat. From their West African home, these snails have spread worldwide.

MASTER INVADER

The African giant snail is one of the top 100 most invasive species in the world.

LARGEST BIRD EGG

5.7 pounds (2.589 kg)
Biggest egg ever recorded

Of all living birds, the common ostrich lays the largest eggs. The biggest one ever recorded was laid in 2008 by a farmed ostrich. It weighed a massive 5.7 pounds (2.589 kg). Within a herd, all the eggs will be grouped together in one nest, and laid on by the dominant female and male of the herd.

FACT BOX   BIG BIRDS

Common ostriches can weigh up to 350 pounds (160 kg).

AFRICA

AFRICAN BUSH ELEPHANT

When it comes to records for heaviest living land animals, the surviving species of elephant top the list. The African bush elephant comes first with males, according to some estimates, capable of reaching weights of more than 7.7 tons (7 mt). African forest elephants and Asian elephants can reach more than 5 tons (5.5 mt), enough to put them second and third on the heaviest animal list. Elephants are vegetarians, eating mostly roots, grass, fruit, and bark. Adult elephants have been known to eat more than 285 pounds (130 kg) of plant material a day.

FAST FACT

Despite their huge size, elephants can run up to 15 miles (24 km) per hour, and maybe even faster!

7.7 tons (7 mt)

SPRINGBOK

When these antelopes were migrating across the western plains of southern Africa they formed the largest known herds of any animals on Earth. These huge aggregations could be 90 miles (145 km) long and contained tens of millions of individual springbok. In the last 120 years, the human impacts of hunting, urbanization, farming, and development have severely impacted their numbers and prevented their migration.

FACT BOX **TEAM UP**

One of the main reasons animals form herds is so they can work together to keep watch and warn each other about any approaching predators.

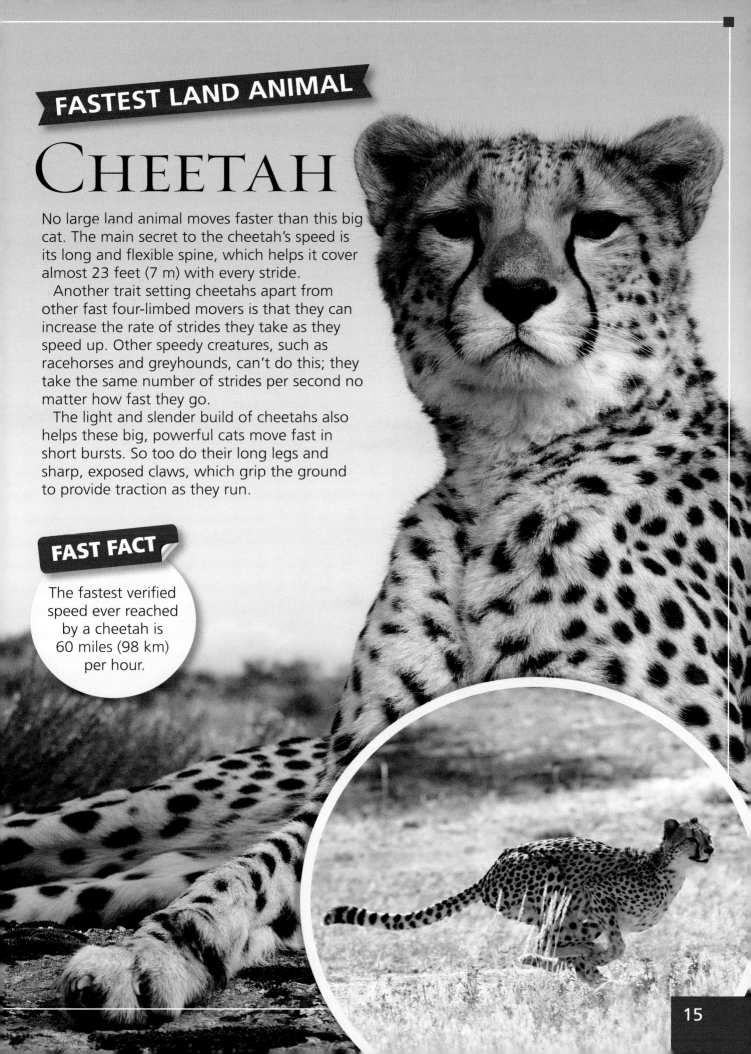

CHEETAH

No large land animal moves faster than this big cat. The main secret to the cheetah's speed is its long and flexible spine, which helps it cover almost 23 feet (7 m) with every stride.

Another trait setting cheetahs apart from other fast four-limbed movers is that they can increase the rate of strides they take as they speed up. Other speedy creatures, such as racehorses and greyhounds, can't do this; they take the same number of strides per second no matter how fast they go.

The light and slender build of cheetahs also helps these big, powerful cats move fast in short bursts. So too do their long legs and sharp, exposed claws, which grip the ground to provide traction as they run.

FAST FACT

The fastest verified speed ever reached by a cheetah is 60 miles (98 km) per hour.

AFRICA

GIRAFFE

Male giraffes can grow to a height of 18 feet (5.5 m), well over 6.5 feet (2 m) more than the next tallest animal, the African elephant. An adult giraffe's neck alone is 6 feet (1.8 m) long and its legs are about the same.

Why are giraffes so tall? One obvious theory is that extreme height gives them an advantage foraging for food in treetops, which shorter animals can't reach from the ground. A more recent theory is that giraffes evolved long necks in males as a secondary sexual characteristic. That means long necks give males a way of competing for mates. You can see just how they do that in a method of fighting called necking, during which males violently swing their necks around at each other.

18 feet (5.5 m) tall

FAST FACT

A group of a giraffes is called a tower.

HIGHEST MAMMAL JUMPER

KLIPSPRINGER

These African antelopes are just 24 inches (60 cm) tall at the shoulder but can jump to a height of 49 feet (15 m), more than 12 times taller than they are. That makes them the highest jumper of all mammals when compared to body size. This extraordinary capability makes it hard for potential predators, such as leopards, hyenas, and baboons, to grab them.

NAME-CALLING

In Swahili, an African language, Klipspringer means "goat of the rocks."

LARGEST FROG

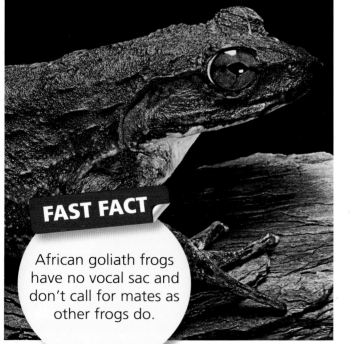

GOLIATH FROG

Most of the world's frog species are small enough to fit neatly on the palm of a human hand. But that's certainly not the case for the goliath frog, which can reach the proportions of a newborn human baby—more than 6 pounds (2.7 kg) in weight!

FAST FACT

African goliath frogs have no vocal sac and don't call for mates as other frogs do.

WITHSTANDS GREAT HEAT

FAST FORAGERS

Sahara Desert ants brave hot desert conditions to scavenge for the carcasses of invertebrates, such as spiders and insects.

SAHARA DESERT ANT

This tiny insect is one of the most heat-tolerant creatures in the world. It's one of a few creatures able to withstand the searing midday heat of the Sahara, which is the hottest **terrestrial** habitat on the entire planet. It leaves its sandy burrow at the hottest time of the day, when the surface temperature can reach 158°F (70°C), but the ant must keep its body below the critical maximum temperature of 131°F (55.1°C) to survive.

OCEANIA

COLDEST BREEDER

EMPEROR PENGUIN

This bird breeds in the coldest place on Earth—Antarctica in winter. There, on the open ice, male emperor penguins huddle together, each with a single egg held up off the ground on their feet and kept warm in a feathered belly pouch. Standing like this, they'll resolutely face months of the worst winter conditions that occur anywhere, including freezing windchills and blizzards. Male emperor penguins won't feed during that entire time, until their partners return from foraging to relieve them of their egg-incubating duties.

FAST FACT

Emperors, the largest of the world's 17 penguin species, reach a height of almost 4 feet (1.2 m).

WEIRDEST DEFENSE

SEA CUCUMBERS

Sea cucumbers, which are relatives of starfish and sea urchins, have one of the most extreme forms of defense against predators. When threatened, these cylinder-shaped creatures can expel their internal organs—particularly their guts—sending them out through either their mouths or the other end, depending on the species. It's a behavior known as evisceration. It's used to scare off the crabs and fish that prey on sea cucumbers. The organs regenerate inside the sea cucumbers within five weeks, and these animals appear to suffer no long-term ill effects.

LARGEST EGG FOR BODY SIZE

KIWIS

The kiwi, a flightless bird found only on the Pacific Island nation of New Zealand, produces the largest egg of any bird in relation to the mother's body size. These eggs are six times bigger than would be expected for a bird the size of a kiwi, and take up about 25 percent of the mother's body. While the ostrich produces the largest egg of any bird, it only takes up about 2 percent of its mother's body.

BIGGEST JELLYFISH

LION'S MANE JELLYFISH

This is not only the jellyfish longest known to science but also a contender for the longest animal on Earth. The biggest known specimen was found dead, washed up on a beach. It had a bell 7.5 feet (2.3 m) wide and tentacles 121 feet (37 m) long. That's long, but possibly not as long as the saltwater bootlace worm.

BIGGEST ANIMAL EVER

98 feet (30 m) long

BLUE WHALE

It's thought that no other animal that's ever lived on Earth has achieved the size of the blue whale, not even the biggest dinosaurs. The largest blue whale on record weighed almost 220 tons (200 mt) and was more than 98 feet (30 m) long. They might be the biggest creatures, but blue whales prey only on tiny crustaceans called krill which they strain from polar waters.

OCEANIA

BIGGEST SHARK

WHALE SHARK

The whale shark, which migrates annually to feed on tiny plankton in waters off the coast of western Australia, is the world's largest fish. Adults can reach a length of more than 32 feet (10 m) and a weight of almost 20 tons (19 mt). These sharks also have the thickest skin of any animal. It is also extremely tough, as it is covered in tiny toothlike scales known as dermal denticles. Not only does whale shark skin help protect these fish from pretty much any potential predator, it also helps reduce drag in the water as they swim.

LARGEST BUTTERFLY

1 foot (30 cm) long

QUEEN ALEXANDRA'S BIRDWING

The largest butterflies in the world are female Queen Alexandra's birdwings. They have a wingspan of almost 1 foot (30 cm). The species is sexually dimorphic, meaning that males and females look very different: the males are smaller than the females and have such different physical markings that they look like a different species. These stunning insects are found only in coastal rain forests in eastern Papua New Guinea and are endangered due to destruction of their habitat.

REPTILE WITH A THIRD EYE

TUATARA

Despite their appearance, these native New Zealand creatures are not lizards. They are the only surviving members of the *Rhynchocephalia*, an ancient group that flourished as long as 200 million years ago. All but the tuatara went extinct around 60 million years ago. Tuataras have a third eye, known as a parietal eye. It's located on the top of the head, though by the time the tuatara reaches four months old it's usually covered in skin and scales. It isn't used for vision, but for regulating temperature and sleep patterns.

FASTEST LIZARD

CENTRAL BEARDED DRAGON

When it comes to the world's fastest lizard, there are at least two contenders. One is the black spiny-tailed iguana of South and Central America, which has officially been clocked running at almost 21 miles (35 km) per hour.

But Australia's central bearded dragon, which races across the landscape at what's estimated to be around 25 miles (40 km) per hour, could prove to be more worthy of the world's fastest lizard title.

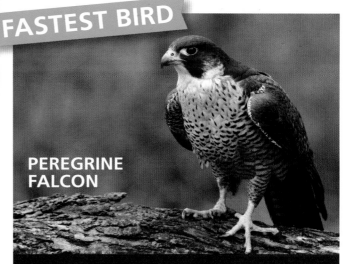

PEREGRINE FALCON

During its hunting dives, the peregrine falcon can reach more than 200 miles (320 km) per hour as it plummets from great heights to swoop in and grab or stun prey. These streamlined, powerfully built birds of prey hunt other birds as well as mammals, such as rabbits. When chasing other birds, peregrine falcons can also fly at great speeds, but not quite as fast as when plummeting using gravity.

DEADLIEST ANT

BULL ANT

There are about 90 species in the Australian ant genus *Myrmecia*, which are most commonly referred to as bull ants. Some of these are known to be potentially harmful to humans. *Myrmecia* have caused more human deaths than any other ants. Altogether, at least six people in Australia have died from **anaphylaxis**—an extreme allergic reaction—after being bitten by *Myrmecia* ants. Five of these have occurred on the Australian island of Tasmania, where at least one study has shown that up to 3 percent of the population is allergic to the venom of the ants. That's twice the level of people allergic to the venom of European honeybees.

HEAVIEST CRAB

TASMANIAN GIANT CRAB

37 pounds (17 kg)

This crustacean is found in the cold, deep ocean waters off southern Australia. Males grow to weights of more than 37 pounds (17 kg), making it the world's heaviest crab. The shells of the largest specimens of Tasmanian giant crabs are up to 18 inches (46 cm) wide.

FACT BOX

SLOW BREEDERS

Tasmanian giant crabs can only mate when they molt, which is when they shed their shells to grow. In adult females this only happens about every nine years.

BEST SENSE OF SMELL

AMERICAN BLACK BEAR

Few animals can challenge this native North American bear's ability to detect smells. Its nose looks large from the outside but what truly sets this creature apart are the folds of tissue lining it. Constantly kept moist, this tissue (known as the nasal mucosa) covers an area 100 times bigger than it does in our human nose. Black bears are estimated to have a sense of smell at least seven times better than the bloodhound, a breed of dog renowned for its ability to sniff things out.

FAST FACT

The black bear's sense of smell allows it to detect a smell at least 1.2 miles (2 km) away. Some scientists think they may be able to detect smells more than 18 miles (30 km) away.

NOT-SO-SPEEDY SLUG

BANANA SLUGS

Slugs and snails have reputations as extremely slow movers! And banana slugs seem to be among the slowest. While the average garden snail moves at a rate of about 30 inches (78 cm) per minute, these bright yellow slugs move at, well, less than a snail's pace: about 6 inches (17 cm) per minute.

LONG LIVES

Banana slugs can live for as long as seven years.

UV VISION

REINDEER

The eyes of most mammals can only detect light in the visible part of the spectrum. But reindeers have a unique visual adaptation that means they are the only mammals that can also see ultraviolet (UV) light. This is believed to be an adaptation to the Arctic environment where they live, as snow and ice reflect a lot of UV light. In contrast, lichen, which is eaten by reindeer, and the bodies of predators absorb UV light. So, being able to see UV light makes it much easier for reindeer to locate their food and avoid predators such as wolves.

SHORTEST LIFE SPAN

MAYFLY

All mayflies have short adult lives, but females of the uncommon *Dolania americana* species take it to the extreme. They live as adults for just five minutes, enough time to mate and lay eggs. After hatching, they burrow into riverbeds where they feed on the larvae of small insects. After about a year as nymphs, males and females emerge and transform into winged adults. Within a few short minutes the next generation is created and the cycle begins again.

HASTY HEARTBEATS

AMERICAN PYGMY SHREW

This is North America's smallest mammal by weight. Adults grow to less than an ounce and maintaining body heat at this tiny size is a constant challenge. It's why these shrews have one of the fastest heartbeats of any mammal (1,200 beats per minute). To sustain such a rapid rate, they need to eat three times their body weight every day, so their life is spent almost constantly foraging for food such as beetles, spiders, and other small invertebrates. They only ever sleep for a few minutes at a time.

STRIPED SKUNK

There are a few animals that use extreme smell as a form of self-defense and skunks are perhaps the best known. These black-and-white mammals don't even try to outrun a threat. Instead, they simply turn their backside at a would-be attacker and spray a noxious substance from large anal glands near the base of the tail. They can spray this oily, hard-to-remove substance out across a distance of almost 10 feet (3 m). Most predators run away rather than take on a skunk.

FAST FACT

The chemicals that make skunk spray smell so bad, which are known as thiols, are also found in rotting flesh and feces.

STINKIEST MAMMAL

LONG LIFE CYCLES

PERIODIC CICADA

Nearly all cicadas spend some of their life underground as juveniles, emerging from the ground to experience a short life as adults. Periodic cicadas are remarkable for their synchronicity (each generation of cicadas emerges at once), and for their life span: They'll spend 13 or 17 years underground as nymphs! They live for four to six weeks as adults. Within two months, they'll be gone and new cicada eggs will have been laid.

MOST ABUNDANT VERTEBRATES

BRISTLEMOUTHS

These tiny **bioluminescent** fish occur in the waters off North America, but also in deep water throughout the world's temperate ocean habitats. Scientists believe that one bristlemouth **genus** (*Cyclothone*) is the most abundant of any on Earth. There are thought to be more individual *Cyclothone* bristlemouths than any other vertebrate— hundreds of trillions of them and possibly even quadrillions (which is thousands of trillions).

SLOWEST FLYING BIRD

AMERICAN WOODCOCK

American woodcocks fly at a respectable rate of 16 to 28 miles (26 to 45 km) per hour when they migrate. But during an elaborate aerial courtship dance performed by males to attract mates, these birds can fly so slowly that they almost stall in midair. During these flights the males will fly as slow as 5 miles (8 km) per hour, the slowest flying speed recorded for a bird. Each male woodcock has a few sites where he performs his courtship flights.

LONGEST HORNS

TEXAS LONGHORN

Sometimes animals live up to their names perfectly! And that's exactly the case with this North American breed of cattle—the Texas longhorn. The average width of the horns on bulls in this breed is 6 feet (1.8 m) from tip to tip and can be even longer in some steers and extraordinary cows. But one steer makes the average horn length seem short. Known as Lazy J's Bluegrass, in 2015, he was acknowledged as the longhorn with the largest horn spread—a massive 9.77 feet (2.978 m) wide.

CAN SURVIVE BEING FROZEN

WOOD FROG

Very few animals can be frozen and not die, and the wood frog is one of them. During the long Alaskan winters it buries itself in the ground and enters a deep state of **hibernation**. It doesn't breathe, its heartbeat stops, and most of the water in its body turns to ice. As spring arrives and it thaws out, bodily functions return and it hops off to begin breeding as soon as it possibly can.

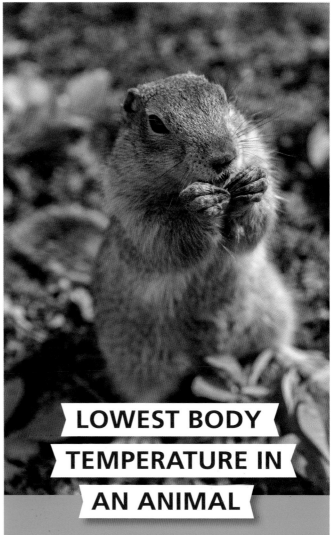

LOWEST BODY TEMPERATURE IN AN ANIMAL

ARCTIC GROUND SQUIRREL

Alaska's Arctic ground squirrel has many adaptations that allow it to survive the harsh Arctic environment. But hibernating, which it does for up to 8 months of every year, is its most effective response. Researchers have discovered that these squirrels drop their body temperature down to the lowest ever recorded for a mammal—to below freezing. This slows the squirrel's **metabolism** down, which helps it to conserve energy so that it can survive its long hibernation, when it doesn't eat or drink.

FACT BOX — MASSIVE LOSS

The Arctic ground squirrel loses about half of its body weight during the eight months it hibernates.

BIG-BEAKED BIRDS

FAST FACT

Toco toucans are mostly frugivores: They eat mainly fruits that they pick from the forest canopy.

TOCO TOUCAN

This is the largest toucan species and it has the biggest beak for its body size of any bird. It's one-twentieth of the toucan's total weight and one-third its total length. Bright but clever coloration ensures these birds are perfectly camouflaged in their homes in Brazil's forest and savanna. But then they seem to go and blow their cover with some of the most varied and noisy vocalizations of any birds. They produce a persistent rattle that sounds like they are having an ongoing conversation. And they create deep croaks that they also repeat incessantly.

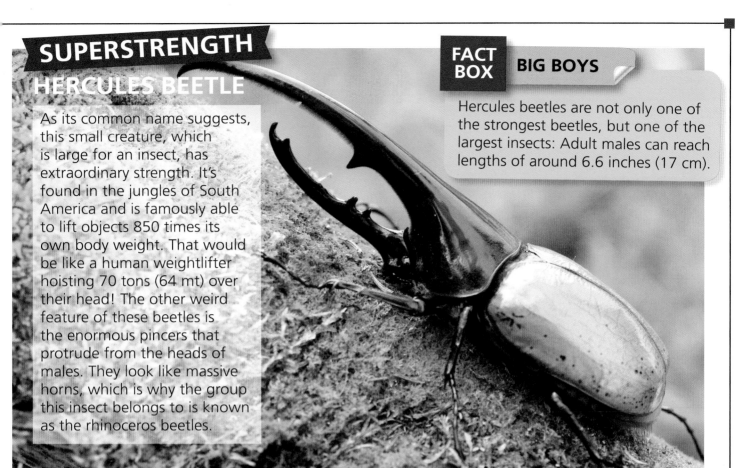

SUPERSTRENGTH
HERCULES BEETLE

As its common name suggests, this small creature, which is large for an insect, has extraordinary strength. It's found in the jungles of South America and is famously able to lift objects 850 times its own body weight. That would be like a human weightlifter hoisting 70 tons (64 mt) over their head! The other weird feature of these beetles is the enormous pincers that protrude from the heads of males. They look like massive horns, which is why the group this insect belongs to is known as the rhinoceros beetles.

FACT BOX | BIG BOYS

Hercules beetles are not only one of the strongest beetles, but one of the largest insects: Adult males can reach lengths of around 6.6 inches (17 cm).

LONGEST MAMMAL TONGUE

TUBE-LIPPED NECTAR BAT

The 3.3-inch-long (8.5 cm) tongue of this bat stretches one and a half times its body length. When compared to the bat's overall body size, it's longer than the tongue of any other mammal. It's only beaten by the ridiculously long tongues of chameleons, a group of lizards found mostly on the African island of Madagascar.

BIGGEST SNAKE

GREEN ANACONDA

Two species vie for the title of biggest snake. The reticulated python is likely to be the longest, but when it comes to sheer bulk, snakes don't get any heavier than a fully grown green anaconda. The largest anaconda ever to be verified weighed 214.2 pounds (97.2 kg) and was 17 feet (5.2 m) long. There are, however, reports of a specimen more than 27 feet (8.5 m) long and estimated to have weighed more than 485 pounds (220 kg).

SOUTH AMERICA

LARGEST RODENT

CAPYBARA

At more than 3 feet (1 m) in length and reaching weights of more than 132 pounds (60 kg), capybaras are many times larger than their close relative, the guinea pig. Capybaras are widespread in lowland habitats of South America near wetlands, swamps, and flooded grasslands where they live partially aquatic lives.

WATER BABIES

Capybaras are strong swimmers that can remain submerged underwater for up to five minutes at a time. They also mate in water.

SMALLEST BIRD

BEE HUMMINGBIRD

This tiny little creature is the world's smallest bird. It reaches a maximum body weight of less than an ounce and a length of less than 2.3 inches (6 cm). It feeds mainly on nectar that it takes from a variety of flower species as it hovers with great precision at the entrances to blooms. The bee hummingbird will also eat insects.

As with other tiny mammals, hummingbirds need a fast metabolism to remain active at such a small physical size. They need to eat up to half their body weight in food every day and drink eight times their body weight in water.

FAST FACT

Hummingbirds are the only birds capable of controlled backwards flight. It's a handy skill for moving back out of blooms when feeding.

GOLDEN POISON DART FROG

We've all heard of deadly snakes, venomous spiders, and jellyfish that can kill you with their stings. But who'd have thought a tiny frog would be up there among the world's most toxic creatures? Adult golden poison dart frogs grow no longer than 2 inches (5 cm) and yet each contains enough poison in its skin to kill up to 10 adult humans. Indigenous people living in South America's forests have for centuries been applying poison from this frog and others like it to the sharp tips of darts used for hunting.

FAST FACT

Medical researchers have developed a synthetic version of a compound called batrachotoxin found in poison dart frog skin that they hope to develop as a powerful painkiller for people.

SOUTH AMERICA

SLEEPIEST ANIMALS

LARGE HAIRY ARMADILLO

When it comes to sleepy animals, this species is up there with the best. Other big sleepers, such as Australia's koalas and South America's sloths, tend to survive on food that's very low in nutritional value, so they don't have the energy to do much else beside eat and sleep. Armadillos are **nocturnal** and tend to forage in the morning and early evening for beetles, termites, and other insects and spend the rest of their time (up to 20 hours a day) in their burrow, not necessarily always fully asleep but certainly hard at rest.

FACT BOX — ALTERNATE SENSES

Armadillos have poor eyesight but a keen sense of smell, which is what they rely on to find food and navigate their way around at night.

STINKIEST BIRD

HOATZIN

South America's swamps seem an appropriate home for the bizarre bird that's widely considered to be the stinkiest– the hoatzin. This bird seems to be a relic species with a lot of peculiar features, and scientists have long been baffled about which other living species are its closest relatives. Hoatzins are herbivores that use bacteria in part of their gut to ferment and help digest the fruit and leaves they eat. Although cattle do a similar thing, it's not seen in any other birds. Unfortunately, the fermentation process and types of leaves hoatzins consume give them a very unpleasant smell of manure!

FAST FACT

Recent genetic research suggests the hoatzin is the only surviving member of a bird group that branched off on its own, just after the extinction of the dinosaurs.

LARGEST TORTOISE

GALÁPAGOS TORTOISE

This, the largest living tortoise species, is also one of the slowest-moving animals for its size. It can usually only make a top speed of just 1 mile (1.6 km) per hour. Males, however, can seem more enthusiastic during the mating season, when they've been tracked traveling as far as 8 miles (13 km) in only two days on treks in search of females. Galápagos tortoises can reach a weight of more than 550 pounds (250 kg).

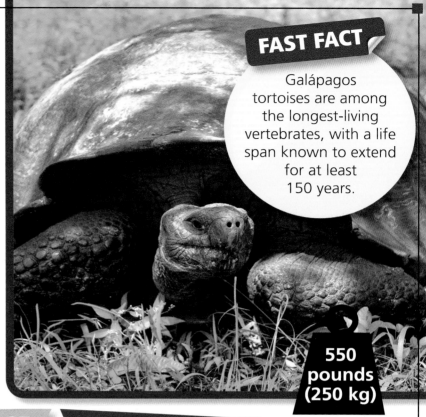

FAST FACT

Galápagos tortoises are among the longest-living vertebrates, with a life span known to extend for at least 150 years.

550 pounds (250 kg)

STRONGEST BITE FORCE

BLACK PIRANHA

For its body size, the black piranha has the most powerful bite of any carnivorous fish. It achieves this by having jaw muscles of an extraordinary size for its overall body weight, as well as having a highly specialized jaw-closing mechanism. This has resulted in a bite force that is equivalent to 30 times its body weight, three times more than the bite force that could be exerted by an American alligator if it were the same size.

UNIQUE FATHERLY CARE

FROG ACTORS

A Darwin's frog will roll onto its back and act dead when it is threatened.

DARWIN'S FROG

There is a range of ways animal fathers get involved in the birth or care of their offspring. But the strategy taken by male Darwin's frogs is one of the most bizarre. After the female lays her eggs in leaf litter, the male fertilizes them and guards them for up to four weeks until tadpoles can be seen wriggling inside the eggs. The male then ingests the eggs and holds them in his vocal sac where they hatch a few days later. He keeps the developing tadpoles in his mouth until they change into tiny frogs and hop out of his mouth.

Glossary

anaphylaxis — An extreme and sometimes deadly allergic reaction.

bioluminescent — Describes the emission of light by a living organism.

camouflaged — Hidden within the surrounding environment.

decibel (dB) — A unit of measurement for the intensity of sound.

genus — A group of closely related species.

hibernation — Spending winter in a safe place.

metabolism — The chemical processes going on inside organisms to maintain life.

migration — Travel from one place to another.

nocturnal — Active at night.

plankton — Tiny organisms floating in fresh or seawater.

predator — An animal that hunts and eats other animals.

satellite tags — Devices that track animals by sending information about their movements to satellites.

savanna — A grassy tropical or subtropical plain.

terrestrial — Living on land.

Index

For More Information

Emminizer, Theresa. *Awesome Ostriches*. New York, NY: PowerKids Press, 2021.

Finan, Catherine C. *Japanese Spider Crab*. Minneapolis, MN: Bearport Publishing Company, 2021.

Rustad, Martha E. H. *Pythons*. North Mankato, MN: Pebble, a Capstone imprint, 2021.

Schuh, Mari C. *Blue Whales*. North Mankato, MN: Pebble, a Capstone imprint, 2021.